MILLION
DOLLAR
JEANS

MILLION DOLLAR JEANS

by Ron Roy

illustrated by Joyce Audy dos Santos

A Unicorn Book   E. P. Dutton   New York

Library of Congress Cataloging in Publication Data

Roy, Ron, date.   Million dollar jeans.

"A Unicorn book."

Summary: Ten-year-old Tommy learns that the lottery
ticket in his jeans pocket is a million-dollar winner,
only to be told that his father has just given the
jeans to a church rummage sale.
[1. Lotteries—Fiction. 2. Jeans (Clothing)—
Fiction] I. Dos Santos, Joyce Audy, ill. II. Title.
PZ7.R8139Mi 1983 [Fic] 82-18320
ISBN 0-525-44047-X

Published in the United States by E. P. Dutton, Inc.,
2 Park Avenue, New York, N.Y. 10016

Published simultaneously in Canada by Clarke,
Irwin & Company Limited, Toronto and Vancouver

Editor: Emilie McLeod   Designer: Riki Levinson

Printed in the U.S.A.   First Edition
10 9 8 7 6 5 4 3 2 1

To all kids who dream about
what's at the end of the rainbow
R. R.

Contents

1 | The Mysterious Woman

WEDNESDAY   1:25 P.M.

Tommy Archer and his best friend, Twig, were bored and broke. They slumped on the grass under Twig's father's cherry tree on an August day hotter than the inside of a basketball player's sneaker.

"What do you want to do?" Tommy's eyelids were at half-mast. His neck was uncomfortable, bent against the tree trunk, but it was too hot to move.

"Go to Hawaii and learn to surf so I can get a job on TV and buy my own plane and . . ."

Twig Collins wasn't only the tallest and skinniest ten-year-old in Hartford, Connecticut. He was also the most talkative.

"*Today*, Twig," Tommy cut in, nibbling on a piece of clover. "What do you want to do today, right now, August whatever it is, 1983?"

Twig stared at the hole in his sneaker through which, if he wiggled hard, he could make a toe appear like a snake. "I don't know. You got any money?"

"Nope. You?"

1

"Ditto, kiddo." Twig twisted into a more comfortable position. "So, as I was saying before I was rudely and crudely interrupted, after I purchase my plane I cruise out to Hawaii, where I acquire me a condominium and fill my swimming pool with Coca-Cola and . . ."

Tommy was on his feet dragging Twig up by a skinny arm. "I'm sorry I asked. Come on, let's go to Arthur's and check out the magazines."

"Okay, at least it's air-conditioned." Twig led Tommy down the flagstone path next to his house. "It's so hot, I can't think."

"I'll say." Tommy gave Twig a shove into the hedges that separated Twig's yard from Mrs. Donkins'.

"You trying to get me killed?" Twig whispered. "She's already threatened to cut off my hair and use it on the bottom of her parrot's cage if I even touch her precious bushes."

Tommy eyed the mass of carrot-colored waves that hung to Twig's shoulders. Twig got teased a lot, but Tommy would have traded his own boring brown hair for his friend's in a second. Not that he'd admit it.

"Before she does, could I have some for my hamster cage?"

Twig planted a sharp punch on Tommy's upper arm.

Tommy raised a sneaker and kung-fu'd Twig's hip.

Twig flew through the air and landed on Tommy's back.

"You boys get away from my shrubs or I'll call the police department!" a voice screeched from Mrs. Donkins' yard.

Tommy and Twig raced down Laurel Street and didn't

2

stop until they were around the corner in front of Arthur's Drugstore.

Wiping their sweaty faces on their T-shirts, they stepped into the delicious coolness of Arthur's air conditioning.

"Ahhh," Tommy sighed, heading for the magazines.

"When I get my plane I'll never stay in horrible Hartford in the summer," Twig said, eyeing the candy bars.

"Where will you go?" Tommy yanked *Batman* from the rack. "It's pretty hot in Hawaii, too."

"Alaska." Twig grabbed *Glider Pilot* and settled himself on the floor. "I'll hunt grizzlies and fish for salmon when they come up to pawn their eggs and catch a baby eagle and . . ."

"*Spawn*, dummy. Pawn means to get rid of something."

"Sure, who doesn't know that?" Twig agreed. "Mother salmons pawn their eggs in the same place every year."

"In a pawn shop?" Tommy asked. "Mother salmons *spawn* their eggs in the same place every year. They don't *pawn* them anywhere."

"Same thing." Twig buried his nose in the magazine. The subject was closed, as Tommy knew well enough after living on the same block as his friend for eight years. If Twig thought he was right, he'd argue till midnight. When he backed off, it was because he realized he'd blown it. Like now.

Tommy was flying through the night, sitting next to Batman in the Batmobile, when he felt Twig's bony elbow in his ribs.

"Get a load of *that*," Twig whispered.

A few yards away stood the tallest woman Tommy had ever seen. Her skin was tanned the color of a new catch-

3

er's mitt and her hair shone like the sun. She wore pink shorts and T-shirt; her arms jingled when she moved because there were about twenty silver bracelets on each one. White sandals revealed toenails painted the color of raspberry Popsicles.

"Wow," Tommy sighed.

"I bet she's a movie star," Twig whispered behind *Glider Pilot.*

"Maybe she's here to act with the Stage Company. Tommy let *Batman* fall to his lap. "Boy, she's beautiful."

"When I get my plane, I'll make a stop in Hollywood and invite all the big stars to—

"Look, she dropped her wallet!"

"I bet it's filled with money." Twig's eyes ballooned with greed. "You knock her down and I'll grab the wallet."

"Don't be stupid, stupid." Tommy slid *Batman* onto the rack. He strolled over and scooped the wallet off the floor. Then he licked his lips and spoke in his most grown-up voice.

"Ma'am, you wopped your drallet."

2 | The Ticket

The woman turned and gazed down at Tommy. "Whah, thank you," she purred. "Ah'm jus' so confused in this big ole town, ah don't know what ah'm doin'."

Tommy stared up into eyes as blue as swimming pools and forgot the English language. He stuck his hand out and the woman took the wallet. She placed her cool, slim fingers on his hot cheek.

"If you aren't the darlin'est li'l thang!" She rummaged through the contents of her wallet and drew out a dollar bill. "Now you jus' take this for bein' such a honey bear."

Tommy managed to cough. "No thanks, I don't want any money." He could feel Twig's laser beam eyes burning holes in the back of his head.

"Wayull, that jus' makes me want to bawl like a baby!" The woman turned to the man standing behind the lottery ticket machine. "Don't you jus' want to have yuh-sef a crah ovah this angel of a boy?"

The man didn't look as if he wanted to do anything of the sort.

6

Tommy felt the blood rush through his veins like mercury in a hot thermometer. He started to turn away.

"Oh no you don't!" The woman yelled so everyone in the store could hear. She turned to the man behind the counter and plunked the dollar bill in front of him. "Ah'll have a ticket please."

The lottery machine cranked out a ticket and Tommy accepted it without saying another word. Already half the people in Arthur's were staring at him.

The woman winked one of her huge blue eyes at Tommy and swished out of his life.

"What's thayat in yo' darlin' li'l hayand, sugah?" Twig crooned. He had been stalking Tommy the whole time. "And why didn't you take the money?"

"You don't take tips when you do someone a favor," Tommy said when he could speak. "It's tacky."

"Tacky wacky," Twig muttered. "We could have bought two Cokes with that buck."

"What do you mean we? You wanted to steal the wallet, remember?"

Twig changed the subject as Tommy knew he would. "So what'd she give you, a ticket to some dumb play?"

"Nope. It's a lottery ticket." Tommy showed Twig the piece of orange cardboard. "Hey, the number's the same as my birthday: 2−9−4−7−3."

"How do you figure?"

"I was born on April twenty-ninth, 1973. Twenty-nine, four, seventy-three. Get it?"

"Cool. So how much do we win?"

"There you go with your we again." Tommy faked a punch at Twig's stomach. "But since you're my best friend, I'll give you half if I win."

Tommy turned to the man behind the counter. "How much do I win with this?"

"Depends," the man said. "You got five numbers. Match one in the same position and you win fifty bucks. Five hundred for two numbers matched in the same places, five thousand for three, fifty thousand for four . . ."

Twig could hardly breathe. "Fifty thou—"

". . . And if you match the five numbers exactly, you win the biggy. One million smackers."

"Dollars?" Tommy gasped.

"I ain't talkin' about baseball cards, kid."

"And I get half!" Twig yelled.

"Why don't you boys take a little walk now," the man said. "You read magazines for free and got a lottery ticket thrown in. How about running along home and doin' your homework?"

"It's summer," Twig piped triumphantly.

"So go mow a lawn."

"Rich kids don't mow lawns." Twig elbowed Tommy. "So when do they call us with the good news?"

"Kids," the man sighed, leaning his hairy arms on the counter, "they don't call. It's on TV every Saturday night. Now scram outa here before I call your mommies."

Outside, they were wrapped in a blanket of heat. Twig perched on top of a fire hydrant. "Me no see cowboys." He shielded his eyes and scouted the terrain. "We go te-pee and eat plenty cookies."

Tommy jammed the lottery ticket into his back pocket and backed up to the hydrant. Twig jumped on and lashed Tommy with an invisible whip.

"Faster, you lazy mule, or I tell everyone about your girlfriend in the pink shorts."

Tommy staggered to the corner and dumped Twig into the bushes. "See you at the tepee."

From deep in the prickly bushes, Twig heard Tommy laughing as he ran down Laurel Street.

3 | Where Are the Jeans?

SATURDAY 9:30 P.M.

The TV announcer flashed a set of perfect white teeth into the camera. He lowered his voice, knowing a couple of million watchers would turn up the volume to hear his next words.

"If you're holding this week's EASY MONEY ticket, here's the moment you've been waiting for."

He turned and handed a fake gold key to a woman in a bathing suit and high heels.

"Sherry will now unlock the revolving cage and pull out a ticket. In just a few seconds, *one* of you will be richer by *one* million dollars!"

"Anyone want anything from the kitchen?" Tommy's mother put down her crossword puzzle and shoved herself off the chair.

"I'll take a beer," Tommy's father said.

"*Shhh.*" Tommy leaned closer to the TV.

Tommy's sister, Stacey, took her thumb out of her mouth. "Can I have some ice cream?"

"You had your dessert. How about a nice apple?"

"Apples are yucky."

"Can you *please* be quiet!" Tommy turned up the volume on the TV. "I'm listening to this."

"An apple or a banana," his mother continued. "Those are your choices."

"Mom, please!" Tommy was on his knees in front of the set.

"REMEMBER, ALL YOU NEED IS A MATCHING NUMBER IN THE WINNING POSITION. BUT FOR ONE OF YOU WITH ALL NUMBERS IN THE RIGHT ORDER, the prize is *ONE MILLION DOLLARS!*"

"Just one cookie?" Stacey wheedled. "I'll eat a banana tomorrow, I promise."

"THANK YOU, SHERRY. AND NOW . . . THE WINNING NUMBERS FOR THIS WEEK ARE 2 . . . 9 . . ."

"I'm sorry, Stacey. No more sweets before bedtime or you'll . . .

"QUIET!" Tommy yelled.

". . . 4 . . . 7 . . . 3. DID YOU GET THAT? I'LL REPEAT IT. THE MILLION DOLLAR WINNER IS 2–9–4–7–3."

Tommy leaped into the air. "I WON. THAT'S MY NUMBER!" he screamed. "I'M RICH! I WON!" He threw himself backwards on the sofa and kicked his feet in the air like an upside-down turtle.

His mother and father stared at their demented son. "What do you mean, you won?" his mother asked. "Won what? And stop jumping on the furniture."

"The million dollars! This lady in Arthur's dropped her wallet and I gave it back and she gave me a ticket and Twig even saw her so he knows. . . ." Tommy stopped

12

to catch his breath. "And I remember the number 'cause it's the same as my birthday. It's the same!"

Tommy raced up the stairs to his room. A minute later he bounded down like a wild boy.

"Where are they?"

"What?"

"My jeans!"

"Which ones?"

"The ones I wore"—Tommy counted on his fingers—"Wednesday. Where *are* they, Mom? The ticket is in the *pocket!*"

"All your dirty things are downstairs next to the washer."

Tommy plunged down the cellar stairs three at a time. His father shook his head and grinned. "I thought you were gettin' me a beer."

Ten seconds later Tommy burst from the basement like a cannonball. "THEY'RE NOT DOWN THERE!"

"Can you please stop yelling? We're in the same room with you." His mother sat down again. "Now, did you look under your bed? In the hall? The bathroom? Next to the—"

"I *looked.*" Tommy bit the inside of his cheek to keep from crying. "Are you sure they were in the laundry room?"

"Honey, you have so many jeans, how am I—"

"They had paint on the knee." Tommy turned to his father. "Remember when I painted the garage door?"

"Then they're at the church." His father stood up. "Guess I'll have to get my own beer." He gave Stacey a little jab in the belly. "I dropped them off with the other things for last night's rummage sale. They were ruined, anyway." He walked into the kitchen.

Tommy went white. He felt the room was spinning. "But

the ticket is in the pocket," he croaked. "Mom, *do* something!"

His father came back with his beer, changed channels and flopped into his Ezee-Back recliner.

Two little dents appeared in Tommy's mother's forehead. "Maybe we should call the church office."

"It's almost ten o'clock," her husband reminded everyone. He looked at Tommy. "When you get to church tomorrow, ask Mrs. Fenner if she remembers your jeans."

"But what if somebody bought them?" Tommy moaned.

His father smiled. "I have a feeling you have nothing to worry about. They're probably still in the box." He looked at his watch. "It's past your bedtime, isn't it, Stacey?"

His mother still looked worried. "Well. Tomorrow will tell, won't it?"

On the TV set, a man in a clown suit ran around the stage smacking at bubbles with a butterfly net. Every time a bubble broke, the clown started blubbering into a huge hankie. He broke every bubble. The audience went wild.

Tommy stumbled out of the room.

"Just one little, tiny cookie?" Stacey teased. "Please?"

4 | Sold!

SUNDAY   7:30 A.M.

Tommy called Twig at seven thirty the next morning.

"What's going on?" Twig yawned into the receiver.

"We won a million dollars."

Twig stopped in mid yawn. There was a pause. "You're kidding, right?"

"I'm not kidding. It was on TV last night. The number they read off was the same as the one on my ticket. *We won!*"

"WE WON A MILLION DOLLARS?"

"Not yet," Tommy said. "That's why I'm calling. The ticket's still in the jeans I was wearing that day. Only my father gave them to the church for some rummage sale. I'm getting them back this morning."

"You mean someone might have *bought* your jeans?" Twig squawked. "With the *ticket* in the *pocket*?"

Tommy's stomach lurched as if he'd been rammed in a bumper car. "Yeah. That's what I mean."

"I don't believe this. The one time in my life I win something, and you go and lose the dumb ticket."

"I didn't *lose* it," Tommy said. "I know where it is. It's in my jeans and I'm getting them back when I go to church. Call me later, okay?"

"Call you?" Twig shouted into the phone. "I'll be sitting on your front steps!"

11:30 A.M.

And he was. When the Archers' car pulled into the driveway four hours later, Twig vaulted the porch railing and practically threw himself into the back seat.

"What happened? Did you get the ticket? Is the number the same?"

Tommy climbed past him and out of the car. "Come on up while I change," he said, ignoring Twig's questions. "We have some work to do."

Upstairs, Twig collapsed on Tommy's bed. Tommy took off his jacket and tie and hung them in his closet. He stepped out of his shoes, then his good pants and hung them next to the jacket. He opened his dresser and selected a T-shirt, then slipped out of the shirt he'd worn to church. It went on a hanger and into the closet for next Sunday. From a hook in the back of the closet, he removed a pair of jeans and climbed into them.

He did it all without looking at Twig and without saying a word.

Twig twitched around on the bed. He gritted his teeth. Finally he exploded. "Are you going to tell me or do I have to strangle it out of you?"

Tommy sat on the edge of his bed with a sneaker in each hand. "Okay. I get there and find Mrs. Fenner; she remembers the box of stuff my father brought in." Tommy pulled on one sneaker but left the lace dangling. "She even remembers my jeans. She says nobody wanted them, so she put them with a lot of other left-over stuff in plastic bags."

Twig sighed and stared at Tommy.

Tommy put his foot on the bed and tied his lace. "And then sold the bags for fifty cents. Each."

Tommy let his foot drop to the floor. "That's the bad news."

Twig closed his eyes. "There's good news?"

"There were three bags," Tommy went on. "Only one got bought. Mrs. Fenner let me look in the other two. My jeans weren't in either of them."

Twig came alive. "You mean whoever bought the bag has your jeans?"

Tommy nodded helplessly. "And Mrs. Fenner remembers who bought it. It's a woman who hangs out at this place where they serve food to people who don't have anything to eat. Her name is Red Sally." He tied his second sneaker. "You ready to go?"

"We're supposed to go find this Sally?" Twig said. "Just like that? We don't even know where this place is."

"I do." Tommy yanked the T-shirt down over his head. "Dad and I brought sandwiches over a couple of times." He lobbed a tennis ball at Twig's head. "You got anything better to do?"

"What if she doesn't give your jeans back? What if she found the ticket herself? What if—"

"What if I punch you in the head? Let's *go!*"

12:15 P.M.

The Friendship Center was serving lunch when Tommy and Twig braked their bikes outside the storefront window.

17

Inside, thirty or forty people were eating or waiting to be served.

"Look," Twig whispered. "Those people are all *old*. I'm not going in there."

"What's wrong with being old?" Tommy said. "They have no other place to eat."

"Why don't they get jobs?"

"Because they're old, dummy. You coming with me or playing Twenty Questions?"

Twig shielded his eyes and peered through the glass. "What if they don't like kids?"

"What a turkey. Okay, stay and I keep the whole million when I find Red Sally." Tommy locked his bike to a light pole and headed for the door.

"Don't get excited," Twig mumbled. "I'm coming." He chained his bike to Tommy's. "But stay near me."

"Don't be such a baby. These people are just like your grandmother."

"That's what I'm worried about."

No one even turned to look when they entered. In the back of the room a man and woman ladled soup from a huge pot into plastic bowls. Sandwiches were arranged in pyramids on the table next to the soup. Plastic spoons and napkins and Styrofoam trays were stacked within easy reach.

Tommy and Twig could have been green Martians and no one would have noticed them.

"What's this Red Sally supposed to look like?" Twig asked.

"How do I know? Look around."

The men and women sat at card tables set up against three walls around the room. Most ate without talking. A few played cards or checkers while they munched and sipped.

In one corner a TV set was on, but no sound came out of it. A long gray cat slept on top with its tail hanging down in front of the screen.

A woman sat watching the silent TV. She was peeling an orange and dropping the peels into a napkin on her lap. Her eyes never left the TV set as she stripped the orange bare.

She wore red sneakers, red running pants and a red sweatshirt with U.S.A. in white and blue across the chest.

Perched on her head was a wig the color of a ripe tomato.

5 | Red Sally

SUNDAY   12:22 P.M.

"That's *her!*" Twig squeaked into Tommy's ear. "What are you going to do?"

Tommy cracked his thumb knuckles with his index fingers. "Wait here."

He cut through the line of people waiting for food, excusing himself, and walked up behind Red Sally. When he stopped, Twig climbed up his ankles.

"What're you *doing?*" Tommy rubbed his heel.

"You left me." Twig swiveled his head around like an owl. "Some guy over there is looking at us funny," he whispered.

"Maybe he's never seen a kid trying to climb into another kid's pocket before."

"How about canning the chitchat so I can hear this!" Red Sally turned away from the TV and glared at Tommy. Her eyes flashed like blue lightning. She popped an orange section into her toothless mouth and swallowed it whole.

20

"The sound's not on," Tommy dared to utter. "How can you hear?"

"I heard you two," the woman snapped, "sneaking around like two dimwits." She moved Tommy aside with a muscular arm and fastened her eyes on Twig. "Is your mouth always open like that?"

Every head in the room turned. Twig prayed for an earthquake. He moved behind Tommy again.

"Did you buy a bag of stuff from the Center Church rummage sale Friday night?" Tommy asked Sally.

"What about it?" she barked.

Tommy backed away, crunching a few of Twig's toes.

"I paid for what I took!" Sally stuck her chin out like a school-yard bully. "If you don't believe me, ask that busybody who took my money."

"Let's get out of here," Twig begged. "Everyone's watching. What if they mug us?"

Tommy ignored Twig's arm tugging. "My dad accidentally put my jeans in the rummage sale and they were in the bag you bought. I just want to buy them back, that's all."

Sally stared, considering. Her eyes blinked like buttons on a calculator. "Five," she said.

"Five what?"

"Five bucks if you want the jeans." Sally licked orange juice from her fingers.

"Okay. Where are they?"

"*Okay?*" Twig honked. "She only paid fifty cents!"

"They're at my place." Red Sally carried the orange peels to a trash can and dumped them. She stood in front of Tommy with her hands on her hips. "Let's see your money."

"It's at my place." Tommy hooked his thumbs into his jeans.

Sally stared down.

Tommy stared up.

It was a standoff. Sally knew it, Tommy knew it and two dozen senior citizens knew it.

Tommy felt like David in the Bible about to fight the giant with a slingshot.

"Wake up your friend," Sally grumbled. "You can have your jeans, but I want the five bucks today."

Tommy nodded. "I'll go home and get it after we get the jeans, okay?"

Sally turned on one big red sneaker and marched out the door.

Tommy untangled himself from Twig and hurried after her. She was already half a block away, heading north. She strode past kids and cats and garbage cans, and Tommy thought about Paul Bunyan stepping over the Rocky Mountains.

"You're crazy," Twig complained, hopping along next to Tommy. "She's leading us off to some deserted place to cut our throats. Somebody will find us floating in the river. Fish eating our eyeballs . . . worms in our noses . . ."

"She's leading us to a million bucks, Twinko." Tommy's eyes gleamed like green marbles. He could picture his bedroom stacked floor to ceiling with wads of money. "But if you want to go home, it's okay with me. And I keep it all, don't forget." He hitched up his pants and walked faster. "Who's afraid of an old lady?"

6 | Sally's Place

SUNDAY 12:31 P.M.

"This old lady can juggle Volkswagens," Twig muttered to himself, but he loped along behind Tommy anyway.

They'd never set foot in this part of Hartford before. There were no houses here. Instead, they were surrounded by brick apartment buildings, most of them housing hundreds of people.

They heard a mixture of languages: Spanish, Vietnamese, Italian. Men sat on front stoops sipping beer and Cokes. Women leaned on pillows in open windows to get a breeze. Transistor radios the size of suitcases filled the afternoon with music.

Kids were everywhere. Big and little, black and white and brown and yellow; they hung on fathers and brothers and uncles who sipped from cans and bottles. They munched cookies and apples in the windows above the street. Mostly they raced over the sidewalks, yelling and kicking cans or throwing balls, enjoying the hot afternoon.

Red Sally moved like a locomotive. When a little kid fell

off his bike, she scooped him into her arms, spit on her hand, wiped the hurt knee and kissed it. She set him on his bike again and he tore away after his friends.

"*Gracias,* Sally!" the boy's mother or aunt called from her window.

"*De nada,*" Sally yelled back.

"Did you see that?" Twig caught up to Tommy. "She wiped spit on that kid's knee. Gross!"

"He stopped crying, didn't he?" Tommy said. "If she gives my jeans back, she can spit on *my* knee. Come on, she's turning a corner."

They slipped into an alley between two buildings. A tall wire fence stood at the end of the alley, barring anyone from going farther. Behind them was Main Street. Except for a few dozen bottles and cans, the place was empty.

"She disappeared!" Twig eyed the boarded-up windows in both buildings nervously. "Maybe she's a witch. Let's get out of here."

"I'm not going anywhere till I get my jeans," Tommy announced. "She has to be somewhere. People don't just vanish."

"Well *I* do," Twig said. "I'm not hanging around while you play hide-and-seek with some old nut."

"WHO'S AN OLD NUT?" The voice seemed to come from out of the ground. Something grabbed Twig by the ankle.

He screamed, squawked and flopped down like a roped calf. "Help!"

Red Sally, with her arm stuck through a basement window, hung on like an octopus.

Tommy started laughing, but Twig was too scared. "Call the police! Call my mother!" He tugged, but Sally held on.

25

Tommy laughed so hard he had to lean against the building.

"Apologize, you little worm, or you'll never see your mother again!" Sally said, winking at Tommy. "I'd feed you to the rats but they like something with a little more meat on it."

Twig stopped thrashing, but he was still shaking as he stared at Sally's face in the ground-level window.

"Well?" Sally barked.

"Well wh-what?"

"Take back what you said."

"I'm sorry," Twig mumbled.

"Better be." Sally drew her arm in and stepped away from the window. Something clanked and Sally's voice came out of the dark. "Come on in, I don't do business in the alley."

Tommy hunkered down in front of the window. "How do we get down there?"

"Feet first," Sally answered. "I'll do the rest."

Tommy sat and scooted forward until his legs were through the window. "Now what?"

"Cross your arms in front of you and lean back."

Tommy followed Sally's orders. He felt her grab his ankles. Then he was sliding from the daylit alley into darkness. His rear end landed on something soft, but he couldn't see a thing. He felt as though he were being swallowed.

Suddenly something big and warm and wet landed on Tommy's face. He started to scream, and the slobbery thing covered his mouth.

Tommy thought he was going to puke.

26

7 | Paws

SUNDAY 12:45 P.M.

Three things happened at once:

The lights came on.

The slimy thing went away.

Tommy's heart started beating again.

He was sitting on a pillow; the floor under it was covered with different colored pieces of square carpeting. The walls were papered with the comics from old newspapers. It looked as if Sally had furnished her place from the side of the road on trash day: two tires on top of each other made a chair; an old mattress covered with fake zebra became a couch; wooden boxes with BUDWEISER BEER stenciled on the side were her tables. There were candles and pillows on the couch, and a plastic Mickey Mouse dangled from the ceiling light pull.

Tommy laughed out loud. It was exactly the kind of room he'd always wanted. It was exactly the kind of room his mother wouldn't let him have.

"Where's the other one?" Sally stood towering over

27

Tommy, holding the collar of a monster. Closer inspection proved it to be a Great Dane, the biggest one Tommy had ever seen. Its tongue hung out like a pink eel. The dog sniffed at Tommy's feet with a huge nose.

"Outside." Tommy stood, keeping his eyes on the dog. "Unless you scared him away."

He turned toward the window and whacked his shin against something hard. It was a coal chute. He'd slid into Sally's living room like a bag of coal!

He yelled into the alley. "It's okay; stick your feet in the window."

One sneaker followed the other, and then Twig was sitting on the pillow. Sally's dog immediately threw one huge paw over his lap. Twig's eyes went blank. He tried to scoot back up the chute like a scared crab.

"He only attacks on command." Sally pulled the dog away from Twig, who huddled on the floor. She yanked the coal chute out from under the window, and then she plopped onto the tire seat. She waved a hand toward the mattress. "Sit there, and don't move too fast."

Twig and Tommy obeyed.

"You live here?" Tommy asked.

"Yep."

"How do you get out the window?"

"I don't. There's a door."

Tommy looked around. "What is this place?"

Sally stroked her dog's ears. "Used to be a coal bin. Upstairs is a liquor store. Me and the owner have an arrangement: Paws and I live here for free and keep the rats away." She glanced cagily at Twig. "The two-legged kind."

"Where do you sleep?" Tommy asked.

"You writing a book?"

Tommy blushed and changed the subject. "Where are my jeans?"

"Over there." Sally motioned toward a black garbage bag in one corner.

Tommy jumped off the mattress.

"DON'T RUN!" Sally yelled. "Paws, no!" Only Sally's quick reflexes stopped Paws from flattening Tommy like a bug.

"He's only trying to play with you." She patted Paws on his big head. "Are you my pussycat?"

Paws flopped onto the floor and rolled over.

Tommy hunched over the plastic bag. He lifted out an old toaster and set it on the floor. Next came a chipped blue vase, then a battered catcher's mitt with a split-open thumb.

Finally Tommy pulled out a pair of jeans and unfolded them. His stomach dropped like an anchor. "These aren't mine," he croaked.

"There were two," Sally said.

"Two what?"

"Two pairs of jeans. One had paint all over the leg so I tossed it."

"You *tossed* it?" Tommy started breathing again. "Where?"

Sally closed her eyes.

Tommy sneaked a look at Twig.

Paws clobbered a cockroach, then ate it.

"You know that First National on Washington Street?" Sally said. Her eyes were still shut.

"Yeah?"

"You know that big Salvation Army box out in front?"

"Yeah?"

Sally opened her eyes. "That's where they are. That's where I threw your jeans."

8 | Sally's Secret Door

SUNDAY   1:05 P.M.

Tommy felt like a balloon losing air. "When?" he asked.

Sally went into her thinking pose again. "Let's see, I got to the church about seven. There wasn't much there, but I bought that bag of stuff and left."

She slipped a finger under her wig and scratched whatever was there. "I had a cup of tea at the White Tower and got back here around nine."

She opened her eyes. "Saturday morning about eight thirty, I walked over to the park. They had a rock concert there Friday night and sometimes people lose money in the grass. I threw the jeans into the Salvation Army box on the way to the park."

Tommy was on his feet, ready to move. He cracked his knuckles against his legs. "You want me to put this stuff back in the bag?"

"No. What's so important about these jeans?" Sally asked, smiling slyly. "They had paint all down one knee."

"There was something in a pocket."

Sally chuckled. "Shoulda looked but I never thought of it."

Tommy nudged the coal chute with the toe of his sneaker. "How do we get out?"

Sally flopped out of her seat and got down on all fours under the window. "Who's first?" she asked.

"What do you mean?" Tommy said.

"Step on my back and climb out."

Tommy couldn't believe she wanted them to use her back as a stepladder. He surveyed the room again. She had said there was a door, but he sure couldn't see it.

"Paws does it all the time," Sally said. "That's how he gets out to do his business, and he weighs ninety pounds." She scrutinized Tommy. "How much do you weigh?"

"Eighty-one," Tommy mumbled. "But you said there was a door. Can't we just go out that way?"

Sally sat back on her feet. "Kids," she muttered. She stepped up to the opposite wall, stuck a finger into a loop of thin wire and pulled. A door swung into the room. It had been wallpapered with comics like the rest of the walls.

"Neat!" Tommy cried. "Where does it go?"

"You'll see, and watch your step. It's dark." Sally closed the window, slid the latch and pulled the Mickey Mouse light string. "Let's go," she said. "Paws, stay."

"Hey, I can't see," Twig cried. "Don't leave me in here!"

Sally's laugh came out of the darkness. "Hold your friend's hand."

Twig lunged and clamped his hands on the loops of Tommy's jeans. They shuffled after Sally. Behind them, the door creaked shut. Then it was so dark even the shadows had shadows.

Tommy sniffed. "What's that smell?"

"Booze." Sally's voice floated in the inky space. "The owner drinks down here. His wife thinks he gave it up ten years ago."

"We're under the liquor store?" Twig said, still attached to Tommy's jean loops.

"Righto. There's about ten thousand bucks worth of stuff right in this room," Sally informed them. "No snitching."

Tommy giggled. "We don't drink."

He felt Sally's big hand on his chest. "Wait here."

Her feet scuffed along the floor. There was a click, a scrape of wood against cement, and then sunlight lit Sally like a big red candle.

"Hurry up before someone sees us." She held the door while Tommy and Twig scurried up the steps that led out of the storeroom.

Outside, just at the top of the steps, a mass of bushes blocked their way. They were about Tommy's height, and when he touched one of the thick stalks it felt prickly, like his father's chin when it was time to shave. Japanese beetles hung all over the plants, eating lacy little holes in the yellow blossoms and broad leaves.

Sally slammed the door behind them and stepped between Tommy and Twig. "Excuse me, gentlemen." She parted the thick stalks of the bushes as if they were blades of tall grass. When she and the boys passed through and turned around, the door was completely hidden by the plants.

"Clever, eh?" Sally said. "Hollyhocks; I planted them from seeds three years ago."

Tommy took a closer look at Red Sally. She'd been living in the basement of a liquor store for at least three years; she kept a Great Dane for a pet; she could be gruff as a grizzly bear, or kind, like now. She was the strangest woman Tommy had ever met.

"Go through that lot," she was saying, pointing west. "Watch the broken bottles. Then left where the sidewalk starts. Bring you right near The Friendship Center."

"Do we have to go back *there* again?" Twig blurted.

"You want your bikes, or do you intend to leave them there?"

"Come on, she's right." Tommy shoved Twig toward the scraggly looking field. He felt funny saying good-bye to Sally. Would he ever see her again? She probably hates kids, he thought a little sadly.

"Thanks a lot." Tommy looked up at Sally and discovered that she was giving him a look, too. "We'll see you. . . . I mean, maybe we'll see you sometime."

Sally gently plucked a Japanese beetle from Tommy's hair. When she opened her fingers, the bug flew into the afternoon. She watched it buzz away, then looked down at Tommy. "No, you won't," she said softly.

She gave them both a little push. "Must be around one o'clock. Better get over to Washington Street if you want your jeans."

She smacked Twig on one shoulder. "And whatever secret you've hidden in the pocket."

They followed Sally's directions through the lot. Before taking the turn, Tommy looked back. Sally was standing where they'd left her. She was watching them, with one arm shielding her eyes from the sun. In the bright light she was a blur of red surrounded by green.

Tommy waved. After a few seconds Sally lifted her hand away from her eyes and waved back. Then she turned and disappeared through her hollyhocks.

9 | The Dark Hole

SUNDAY 1:35 P.M.

"Why me?" Twig stared at the black hole in front of him. "They're your dumb jeans."

They were in front of the Salvation Army box on Washington Street. The box was made of metal and painted bright red with a red and white Salvation Army seal on the front; it was the size of a small bathroom and had a locked door for taking out the stuff that people donated. Above the door was a slot for dropping in clothing.

It was through this slot that Tommy planned to drop Twig.

"Because you're skinnier than me." Tommy measured Twig with one eye squinting. "All you have to do is jump in and find my jeans." He grinned. "Half a million bucks?"

"What if someone sees me?" Twig glanced around at the Sunday food shoppers streaming in and out of the First National. "This is stealing."

"It's not stealing," Tommy said. Then he added, "They're my dumb jeans."

"Okay, gimme a boost," Twig grumbled. They laid their

bikes on the parking lot tar. Tommy locked his fingers together to make a foothold, and Twig stepped on Tommy's hands. Twig held on to the rim of the clothing slot with one hand while the other grabbed Tommy's hair.

"Hey, I'm not a horse," Tommy yelled. "You're hurting my hair!"

"Lift!" Twig hollered.

"Climb!" Tommy yelled back. "And get your thumb out of my eye!"

He shoved, and Twig's head and shoulders disappeared through the slot. He hung half in and half out, as if he were being eaten by a red robot.

Twig's voice came out of the hole. "I'm stuck!"

Tommy shoved harder.

Twig didn't budge. "My buckle is caught on the edge," he yelled from inside. "And it's dark in here."

"Use your hands to lift off while I push," Tommy ordered.

Twig raised his stomach off the edge of the slot and Tommy gave one more hoist. Twig's legs and feet disappeared. There was a thud. He was inside the box.

Tommy stared up at the hole. "How're you doing?"

A woman carrying a sack of groceries smiled at Tommy. "Why, I'm doing fine, thank you. And how are you, young man?"

"Fine, thanks, heh-heh-heh," Tommy said. He waited until the woman walked away, then kicked the side of the box. "Can you hear me?" he whispered as loud as he could.

"Yeah." Twig's voice floated out of the hole, muffled and faraway sounding. "I can see pretty well now."

"What's in there?" Tommy shifted from one foot to

the other. He wiped sweat from his face with his T-shirt.

"Not much," Twig answered. "Some plastic bags, mostly."

Tommy thought about Sally tossing the jeans into the box yesterday morning. She hadn't said anything about using a plastic bag. "The jeans will be loose," he said.

The heat in the parking lot was frying Tommy's head. "What's *taking* so long?" he asked.

Twig didn't answer. Tommy stood on tiptoe and moved closer to the clothing slot. "Twig? What the heck are you doing?"

"I'm searching under these bags and I—" Twig screamed. It started like a moan, then got louder and higher, like the time Tommy's sister's cat caught its tail in the refrigerator. Then it stopped.

Tommy chinned himself on the slot edge, but he still couldn't see inside. *"What's the matter!"*

No answer.

"Twig! Are you all right? What's going on?"

Nothing came out of the slot but a fly.

Tommy didn't know what to do. He kicked his feet against the hot metal, trying to climb higher.

Suddenly two hairy hands grabbed him around the shoulders. Tommy screamed. He was paralyzed. A horrible face with black lips and furry cheeks emerged from the dark hole.

10 | Monkey Boy

SUNDAY 1:50 P.M.

Tommy stared into the face of King Kong.

"Me no hurt boy," the black lips said. "Me nice monkey."

"Twig!" Tommy snatched the mask off Twig's head and dropped to the ground. "You're dead when you get out of there!"

"Neat, huh?" Twig's face was flushed and sweaty. He was grinning like a fool. "Who's dumb enough to get rid of cool stuff like this?" He wiggled one set of hairy fingers.

"You're never gonna find out. When I get . . . Oh, forget it."

"Me like boy. Boy like monkey?"

Tommy clenched his jaws so he wouldn't smile. It didn't work.

"Okay, I'm not mad at you. But where are the jeans?"

Using his teeth, Twig pulled the right gorilla mitten off and tossed it to Tommy. "They're not in here." He yanked the other mitten off and threw it after the first. "Everything else but."

He threw one leg over the rim of the slot, balanced himself till the other leg was out, then jumped to the ground.

Tommy swallowed hard. His fist hit the metal of the Salvation Army box. "Are you sure?"

"Honest, Tom," Twig said. "Shoes, ratty old sweaters, some little kids' stuff. No jeans at all. I searched under everything."

Twig took back the mask and mittens. "Boy, wouldn't it be neat if I had the rest of this suit? I'd put it on and wait for Mrs. Donkins to water her darling bushes." He cackled at the thought of his neighbor finding a gorilla in her snapdragons.

Tommy wasn't enjoying the joke. He was standing very still, staring into space.

"I suppose the jeans could be inside one of the bags," Twig offered.

Tommy shook his head. "Sally said she threw in the jeans. She'd have told us if they were in a bag." He picked up his bike. "Come on, let's take off."

They headed out of the parking lot. Twig had stuffed the mask inside his T-shirt, but wore the mittens. He looked like a fat werewolf.

Next to him, Tommy rode silent and depressed.

"Wanna sleep over tonight?" Twig had never seen his friend in such a bad mood.

"I just got an idea." Tommy ignored the invitation to sleep over. "We're going to the Salvation Army."

"There really *is* such a place?" Twig cracked a grin. "With soldiers and tanks?"

"What a donkey." Tommy lurched his handlebars to avoid hitting a can in the gutter. "Sure it's a place. Where do you suppose all that stuff in the boxes ends up? And I bet that's where my jeans are. Let's go."

"It's Sunday, Tom," Twig said. "They're probably closed."

Tommy executed a U-turn, terrifying the driver behind them.

"Now where're you going?" Twig said, following.

Tommy didn't answer. He pulled back into the parking lot and headed for the phone booth. He left his bike on the ground and pushed open the booth door, fishing in his pocket for a dime. When he reached for the telephone book, it was missing.

He dropped his sweaty dime into the coin slot, dialed, and asked Information for the number of the Salvation Army.

Twig sat outside the booth.

"They're closed," Tommy muttered, pushing the door open and grabbing his bike.

"It's Sunday," Twig said again.

"I *know* it's Sunday!"

"Can't we go tomorrow?"

Tommy nodded absentmindedly. He polished the chrome handlebars with the front of his stretched-out T-shirt.

"Tom? How does the stuff get from these boxes to the Salvation Army place?"

"I don't know. Maybe I better just give up and forget the whole thing."

"We can at least try," Twig said. "We'll go first thing tomorrow."

"Hmph."

"If you sleep over, we can use my tent."

Silence.

"And I'll make fudge."

Tommy's eyes brightened. "You know how to cook fudge?"

Twig looked hurt. "Do I know . . . I can read a cookbook, can't I? I can turn on a stove, can't I?" He looked at Tommy as if he were talking to a three-year-old. "Of *course* I know how to make fudge!"

11 | Floating Fudge

SUNDAY   8:30 P.M.

The tent was almost the same shade of orange as Twig's hair. Tommy tossed his sleeping bag through the flap and went to find his friend.

Twig was sitting on the kitchen floor chewing on a wad of his hair pulled across his cheek and under his nose. He was staring at the pile of cookbooks that he'd pulled from the shelf under the spice rack. "I don't know which one to use," he muttered.

Tommy stood over Twig for a few seconds, then yanked a book from the pile and dropped it on the kitchen table. "This one." He draped himself over a chair and let out a long sigh. "Where are your folks and Freddy?"

"Next door playing bridge. They took the monster with them." Twig sat across from Tommy and flipped the cookbook open. "The last time I cooked something, Freddy tried to help and stuffed a raisin up his nose."

Tommy wasn't listening. He was lighting a stick of dynamite at the back door of the Salvation Army building.

44

He was crawling through the smoke and splinters, searching for his jeans.

He let out another sigh and plucked a grape from the bunch on the table. "So what happened?"

Twig stared at Tommy blankly. "What, what happened?"

"To Freddy."

"Oh." Twig found Fudge in the index and flipped the pages backwards. "Mom took him to the Emergency Room. She was a wreck and Freddy was crying like crazy. When the doctor shined his light up Freddy's nose, the raisin was gone."

Twig found the fudge recipes and ran his finger slowly down the page.

"Gone? The raisin just disappeared?"

"The doctor told Mom it probably went down his tube because he was crying so hard." Twig shook his head. "Jeez, there's a million kinds of fudge. Listen: 'Chocolate Puffy Fudge, Brown Sugar Fudge, Marshmallow Fudge, Twenty Minute Fudge' . . ."

"What tube?" Tommy asked. He slapped his hand over the fudge page.

"Huh?"

"What tube did the doctor say the raisin went down?"

Twig looked up from the book. He opened his mouth like a hippo and pointed down his throat with his head tipped back. He tried to say something while pointing, but he sounded as if he were choking.

Tommy leaned across the table and peered into Twig's mouth. "I don't see any tube," he said, "just that gross

45

pink thing hanging down." He sat back in his seat. "And all your fillings."

"Well, smartso, the doc *said* there's a tube where the stuff from your nose runs down your throat, like when you have a cold. You know, when your nose is all filled up with—"

"Shut up." Tommy grabbed the cookbook and studied the fudge selections. But he couldn't concentrate on recipes. "Do you think this is gonna work?" he asked Twig.

"Sure, all we have to do is follow the directions in the book."

"No, Twink, I mean finding my jeans at the Salvation Army." Tommy rested his arms on the book and plunked his chin on the backs of his hands. "If they ever got to the Salvation Army box to begin with."

"We can go look tomorrow, anyway." Twig slid the cookbook out from under Tommy's arms. "What do we have to lose?"

"Nothing." Tommy closed his eyes as if he were in pain. "Only a million bucks."

"You know who you sound like?" Twig asked.

"You?"

"No, my grandmother. You know what she says when someone gives her a present? 'Where will I keep it?' or 'Now I have one more thing to dust.' She's really a lot of fun to be around, you know?"

Twig scanned the page in front of him. "Here we go, 'Million Dollar Fudge, page 279.' "

"Lemme see." Tommy snatched the book again and looked at page 279. " 'Million Dollar Fudge.' Hmph. I never heard of it."

Twig was out of his chair. "You never heard of a lot of things, like my brother's tube that sucked down the raisin." He started jamming the rest of the cookbooks back onto the shelf.

Tommy ignored the remark and studied the recipe. "First we need a nine- by nine-inch pan."

Twig pulled open the drawer under the oven and rattled around until he came up with a shallow square pan. "Got it. What next?"

Tommy wiggled his finger around in his ear. "It says the pan should be well oiled." He looked at Twig. "What kind of oil?"

Twig studied the book upside down. "You sure it says oil? Maybe they mean boil or foil or . . ."

"It says oy-yull," Tommy insisted.

Twig set the pan on the table and walked over to the shelf above the cookbooks. "Hey, what's this?" He showed Tommy a bottle of yellow liquid. " 'Olive Oil,' " he read from the label. "What do you think?"

"Must be the stuff," Tommy said, nodding wisely. "I think my mom's got some of that, too. Now," he said, lowering his eyes to the book, "we need 'twelve ounces semisweet chocolate,' whatever that means, 'one cup miniature marshmallows, two cups sugar' . . ."

While Tommy read, Twig raced around the kitchen yanking things from shelves and drawers.

Tommy perused the pile of ingredients in front of him on the table. "Salt? Who ever heard of salt in fudge?" He tossed the salt box to Twig. "Must be a mistake."

He picked up a large, partly eaten chocolate bar. "What's this?"

"It's the only chocolate I can find," Twig said. "Not to worry. How much of this stuff do I need?" He was already pouring olive oil into the pan.

Tommy watched the yellow liquid gurgle out of the bottle, flow across the bottom of the pan and ooze up the sides.

"That looks about right. Next you 'Combine the sugar, marshmallows and chocolate in a three-quart pot and stir to blend well.' " He stuck his finger between the pages and looked up. "What's a three-quart pot?"

Twig reached under the counter and came up with the one his mother used for making spaghetti sauce. "How's this?"

"Excellent. Now, 'Place over medium heat and bring to a boil.' "

"Bring what to a boil?" Twig held the pot in one hand and the pan of oil in the other. "I don't get it. Bring the pot to a boil? Bring the oil to a boil? *Boiled oil?* Read it again, Tommy."

8:52 P.M.

Tommy read the last instruction. " 'Pour mixture into well-oiled pan and let stand, chilled, until firm; then cut into squares and serve.' "

He slapped the book shut and stood by Twig's elbow to watch the pouring. Only it didn't pour. The mixture stayed in the bottom of the pot as still and permanent as glue.

"Maybe it's firm enough already," Tommy offered, eyeing the congealed mess.

"The book says pour it into the well-oiled pan and that's what I'm gonna do." Twig slammed the pot on the counter

48

a few times, then checked the contents for pourability. Only one brown bubble heaved up and flattened.

"Get me a wooden spoon."

Tommy slapped it into Twig's outstretched hand.

"And a knife."

"Knife." *Slap.*

"Sponge. *Quick!*"

The spoon and knife dislodged about a pound of brown goop, and the oil washed over the sides of the nine-by-nine pan.

Tommy pushed the escaping oil into the sink with the sponge.

The boys stared at their creation. It was a brown iceberg floating in a yellow sea.

"Doesn't look like my grandmother's fudge," Tommy muttered. He poked the iceberg with one finger.

"It looks *better* than *my* grandmother's," Twig said.

"So now we chill this stuff?" Tommy asked. "Isn't it hard enough already?"

"Open the fridge." Only a little of the oil slopped over the sides of the pan as Twig transferred the quivering mess into the refrigerator.

9:35 P.M.

Later, after the comics had all been read and traded, Twig rolled over in the tent. "Tom? You awake?"

"Who wants to know?"

"Me. I'm hungry."

Tommy smiled in the darkness. "Fudge?"

Twig nodded. "Fudge."

They tiptoed over the grass, climbed the back steps and slipped into the house.

50

The refrigerator opened with a cool *whoosh*. Twig set the fudge pan on the counter. He jabbed at the floating lump with his finger. It tipped, then righted itself, rippling the oil.

Tommy carried the pan into the bathroom.

Twig heard a splash just before the toilet flushed.

Tommy came back and slid the empty pan into the sink. "Mission accomplished."

Twig grinned. "Over and out." They grabbed a box of crackers and slipped through the door, crossed the dark lawn and crawled into the tent.

9:45 P.M.

"Tom?"

"What?"

"Sorry about the fudge."

"That's okay. Next week I'll buy us a candy store."

" 'Night, Tom."

" 'Night, Twig."

12 | At the Army

MONDAY   8:59 A.M.

Tommy and Twig ate a fast breakfast and biked to the Salvation Army office on Homestead Avenue. The doors were still locked, but through the glass they could see employees moving around.

An old man in a guard's uniform approached the door from the inside and held up a finger. "One minute," he mouthed.

Tommy smiled at the guard. He wiped his wet palms on the seat of his jeans, conscious that his heart was beating a lot faster all of a sudden. In his mind he was counting stacks of one-hundred-dollar bills. He wondered what it would look like, a million bucks, dumped in his bedroom.

Twig stood next to Tommy on the steps. For once he wasn't jabbering. He kept licking his lips and taking deep breaths.

The door swung open. "Morning," the guard said. "Help you?"

Tommy had rehearsed what he would say. "I need to

speak to someone about a lost article of clothing. I have to find it today or my family is going to be very upset."

Twig stared. They hadn't even told Tommy's mother where they were going. Tommy had told Twig his parents still didn't believe the ticket in his missing jeans was the winner.

"Don't know anything about lost articles," the guard said, hustling the boys in off the steps. "You'll have to ask in the office. Mind your feet, now."

Wearily, as if he'd made this trip a thousand times, the guard led Tommy and Twig up some carpeted steps and along a corridor with glassed-in offices on both sides.

At the end of the corridor, they saw a woman with white hair and red lips sitting in a glass cubbyhole.

The guard stooped over and spoke through a window in the glass. "Boys lost something, Dorothy." He turned back to the boys. "Dot runs this place," he whispered so the woman could hear every word. "Her trouble is she hates people." He winked and shuffled away.

Behind the window, Dorothy reached one hand toward her coffee mug while the other groped for a lit cigarette. She sucked in some smoke, blew it out through her nose and took a swig of coffee.

She looked up with the cigarette dangling from one corner of her mouth and her eye squinting to keep out the smoke. "The only person I even come *close* to hating," she muttered with the cigarette dancing, "is that old monkey."

She blew another coil of smoke and smiled. "What did you lose?"

Tommy told her how his father had given his jeans to

the church and about how Red Sally had dumped them into the box. "My friend and I searched the box yesterday, but we didn't find them. We thought they got delivered here."

Dorothy was shaking her head before he was through talking. "If you don't know how much stuff comes into this place every day, you're in for a surprise."

She let herself out of the cubbyhole and marched down the hall, signaling for Tommy and Twig to follow. "A man came in last week practically having a stroke. Said his wife gave us his best camel's hair coat and he wanted it back." Dorothy chuckled at the memory. "Poor guy."

"Did he find it?" Twig asked.

"Nope."

The golf ball that had been stuck in Tommy's throat all morning turned into a shot put and dropped to his stomach.

Dorothy stopped in front of a door with a small sign fastened to the wood. In gold letters the sign said, C. C. FALLON, DIRECTOR. She knocked lightly and pushed the door open, letting the boys pass under her arm. She patted Twig's hair as he moved past her. "Good luck, honey."

Mr. C. C. Fallon worked in a jungle. Plants hung from the ceiling and grew out of pots on the floor; they sat on shelves and benches and tables; flowering plants sprouted from red clay pots and green plastic pots and black metal pots. There were tiny white blossoms peeking out of dirt-filled seashells; an enormous tree rose from a wooden tub and spread its branches over a whole corner of the room.

A man stood on a stepladder with his back to the door. He looked like a monkey in its natural habitat. He held a green watering can in one hand. "Here you are," he said. "I'll bet you're thirsty this morning."

"No, thank you," Tommy said.

The man almost fell off the ladder. "Who are you?" His face was the color of strawberry ice cream.

"Tommy Archer."

"Twig Collins."

"How did you get in here?"

"The lady let us in," Tommy mumbled.

"Dorothy?"

They nodded.

The man blinked, setting the watering can on the top step of the ladder. "Oh, I see." He descended to the floor backwards, holding on to both sides of the ladder.

"I'm Charles Fallon." He shook hands with each of the boys. Then he smiled, for the first time. "I guess you heard me talking to my plants. I do it all the time. Do you think that's crazy?"

He motioned to a pair of chairs without waiting for an answer. Then he sat and folded his hands on his desk.

C. C. Fallon smiled. "You've lost something, right?"

13 | C. C. Fallon

MONDAY 9:06 A.M.

Tommy's mouth fell partly open. "How did you know?"

Mr. Fallon straightened four yellow pencils on his blotter. "Every week someone comes in looking for a watch or a favorite sweater or a pair of shoes that have been donated to us by mistake." He smiled at Tommy and Twig. "I don't talk *only* to plants."

"Do they get their stuff back?" Twig asked.

"Some do, some don't," Mr. Fallon said. "We're a big operation. Items coming in one day are usually gone again that same evening. We have to be fast or we'd be neck-deep in people's discards."

"Where does it all go?" Tommy asked the question but he really didn't want to know. He wanted to go to the bathroom.

"We sell it from our stores. We have eight in Hartford alone. Our drivers empty out the red boxes every day, and bring the items here where they are sorted and priced. Then they're delivered to the stores." Mr. Fallon came around and leaned on the front of his desk. "Now, what did you lose?"

Tommy repeated the story of the rummage sale and Sally and hoisting Twig into the Salvation Army box on Washington Street. He left out the part about the lottery ticket.

Mr. Fallon raised, then dropped, his eyebrows and grinned. "There must be something special about these trousers, but that's your business. When did they get dropped into the box?" He turned and picked up a small desk calendar from his blotter.

"Saturday morning."

"About eight thirty," Twig added.

"Hmm." Mr. Fallon squinted his eyes. "Since the weekend was involved, there's a small chance that your pants are still here." He slipped out of an apron and into his suit jacket, then moved to the door. "Shall we have a look?"

He led the boys down the same corridor they'd passed through earlier. They stopped at a door with an EMPLOYEES ONLY sign on it. "This is where it all happens," Mr. Fallon said. He opened the door and let the boys walk in first.

The room was as big as a football field. A corner near them was stacked with bulging burlap bags. "Those are filled with the clothing our drivers brought in this morning," Mr. Fallon said. He noticed Tommy's eyes widen. "Don't worry, yours isn't in that pile if it went into the red box on Saturday."

They continued walking. Mr. Fallon pointed toward about twenty people standing along one wall emptying bags of clothes onto the floor. "Those people are our sorters and pricers."

They moved a little closer. Tommy watched one of the

sorters pick a white sweater from the pile; she held it up, looked at both sides and under the arms, then tossed it into a box. The box was one of about ten along the wall. Each box had numbers painted on the front side. The other sorters were throwing pieces of clothing into the boxes.

"Those numbers are the prices that will be stapled to the clothes before they reach the stores," Mr. Fallon told the boys. "Everything of the same price goes into the same box. Sweaters, for example, are three dollars, and so are men's dress shirts. They both go in the three-dollar box."

"How much do you get for monkey disguises?" Twig asked suddenly.

Mr. Fallon looked confused. "I don't understand."

Twig explained about the mask and mittens he took from the collection box.

Mr. Fallon laughed. "Our specialty items go into our own store right here on the premises." He winked at Tommy. "And we usually get fifty dollars apiece for costumes."

Twig's face dropped. "Fif—"

"But we'll talk about that in my office." Mr. Fallon guided the boys to another area of the room. He stopped in front of a huge, black machine with an empty space in the middle. Workers were dumping clothes into the hole. When it was crammed full, one of the workers flipped a small switch on the wall and the machine began shuddering. A loud hum filled the air.

The rest happened so fast Tommy wasn't sure what he'd seen. Two large jaws crushed the clothes into a tight bundle and wires came out of nowhere to wrap around the bundle. Two workers grabbed it and dragged it off the machine into a corner where a forklift operator waited to carry it away.

"Those bales will be sold to rag dealers," Mr. Fallon explained. "The clothes are no good; badly ripped or stained, usually. The rag dealers cut up the clothes and sell the pieces to manufacturing companies for cleaning rags."

"My jeans had paint on them!" Tommy cried.

"You're looking for jeans?" Mr. Fallon said. "Why didn't you say so?"

"I didn't think it mattered," Tommy said. He watched as the workers loaded the baling machine again.

"It does matter. Jeans go through a different procedure." Mr. Fallon led the boys toward the exit. "We sell denim overseas where we get more money. How much paint was on these jeans?"

"A lot," Tommy said. "I was painting the garage door and I kneeled on the brush." He had a sick feeling that his lottery ticket was on its way to Africa.

When they were in the corridor again, Mr. Fallon put his hand on Tommy's shoulder. "Don't look so down in the dumps. I think I know where your jeans are."

14 | Tommy Believes

MONDAY 9:30 A.M.

Mr. Fallon picked up his phone and dialed one digit. "Dorothy, please bring me the number of that man on Fish Fry Street who buys the jeans. Potter, that's right. Thank you."

Tommy sat on his hands so he wouldn't eat his fingernails. Twig looked dazed.

"This Mr. Potter came in one day and asked if we'd sell him all the jeans and other denim we get in. When I told him we sell what's in good condition overseas, he asked to buy what we couldn't sell. I agreed." Mr. Fallon pointed one of his yellow pencils at Tommy. "I think Mr. Potter has your jeans."

"Far out!" Twig whooped.

"Can I use your bathroom?" Tommy asked.

Mr. Fallon pointed toward a small door leading from his office.

"What does Mr. Potter do with the jeans?" Twig asked.

"I never asked him," Mr. Fallon said. He stretched his

hand out as Dorothy came in with a piece of paper. "Thanks, Dottie. Address, too? Good."

Mr. Fallon dialed the number, then cupped one hand over the phone as Tommy came back in. "He comes by most nights just before we close." He glanced at the paper in his other hand. "It seems Mr. Potter is a tailor."

Mr. Fallon spoke into the phone. "Mr. Potter? Charles Fallon at the Salvation Army office. Did you come by Saturday evening for your regular pickup? You did." Mr. Fallon winked at the boys. "Well, I have two young men in my office looking for a pair of jeans. May I send them by to see if it's among what you took on Saturday? Fine, and thank you, Mr. Potter."

He slid the paper across the top of his desk. "Here's the address. Are you fellows walking?"

"We have our bikes," Tommy said, taking the paper. "Where's Fish Fry Street?"

"Let's look." Mr. Fallon showed the boys a map of Hartford hanging on the wall. "These red pins show the locations of all the red collection boxes; the yellow pins represent our eight stores."

"What's the blue pin?" Twig asked.

"That's our office, where we are right now. And this," he said, sliding his finger three inches, "is Fish Fry. I don't think you'll have a problem. Simply turn right out front, then left on North Main. Three blocks on your right should be Fish Fry Street."

"We really appreciate your helping us," Tommy said.

"Glad to do it." Mr. Fallon shook hands with the boys. "But thank me after you have your jeans back."

He hung his suit coat on its hanger and slipped the apron

61

loop over his head. "My plants are calling me. Good luck to you."

"What about the monkey costume?" Twig said.

"Ah, I'd almost forgotten. Why don't we make that a gift to you?" Mr. Fallon said. "When you get home maybe you'll find some things to drop into that red box on Washington Street. Fair enough?"

"Great!" Twig said. "I'll get a bunch of stuff from my relatives, too."

"That will be wonderful." Mr. Fallon held his door open. "Good luck again, to you both."

The boys waved to Dorothy as they hurried down the corridor. She waved back through a haze of cigarette smoke.

While they were twisting their combination locks, Twig stopped and looked at Tommy's back. "Now don't get mad, but I just want to ask one question, okay?"

"You made me miss a number," Tommy said. "And I'm not promising anything."

"Okay. What if your jeans never left the church with Red Sally? What if they weren't in the plastic bag at all. Or what if Sally lied?"

Tommy twisted his lock again. When it popped open, he hung the lock on a belt loop and wrapped his chain around his bike seat. "I believe her, that's all," Tommy said. Then he climbed on his bike and pedaled toward Fish Fry Street.

15 | Fanny's Shop

MONDAY 9:41 A.M.

By the time Twig caught up, Tommy was halfway down Homestead Avenue. Five minutes later they were in front of Fanny's Tailor Shop on Fish Fry Street.

It was small, just two plate-glass windows on either side of a door. A sign in the left window said that Fanny's could also remove stains, fix zippers and store fur coats.

But Tommy was staring at the right window, so Twig looked, too. Another sign, this one bigger, said USED JEANS SOLD HERE—LIKE NEW—GOOD PRICES.

Behind the sign, displayed on coat hangers suspended on thin wires, was an assortment of blue denim. There were vests and shirts and jeans and skirts and visors and book bags. Everything had been worn before, but Fanny's had repaired and cleaned and pressed it all to near perfection.

Inside, a woman sat at a sewing machine stitching something on a cowboy shirt. She smiled through the glass.

"Do you see what I see?" Tommy rested his head against the window. He felt nauseous, like the time he had heat stroke at camp.

Twig nodded. He couldn't think of a thing to say.

A bell tinkled when they entered. The woman left her sewing. "Can I help you?"

"Is Mr. Potter here?" Tommy asked. He fought the temptation to let his eyes roam around the shop. His jeans might be only a few feet from where he was standing. What would happen to a lottery ticket in a washing machine, he wondered.

"My husband is at the bank," Mrs. Potter said. "Is there something I can do?"

"I'm looking for some jeans."

"What size are you?" The woman reached for the tape measure around her neck. "Let me measure your waist."

"No, they're mine already. I lost them. I mean, my father gave them away, and I think they went to the Salvation Army. Mr. Fallon called . . ."

"Oh, you're the ones he called about a few minutes ago."

Tommy nodded.

"Can you describe your jeans?"

"They're blue," Tommy said lamely.

"With white paint on one knee," Twig added.

"Blue with white paint," Mrs. Potter repeated. "I remember those. They came in with the batch my husand picked up Saturday evening." She shook her head at Tommy.

Tommy swallowed the smile that had almost made it to his lips.

"We never fool with paint," Mrs. Potter was saying. "I threw those out."

She threw those out. Tommy wanted to cry.

"When?"

64

"Where?"

"Saturday night before we closed . . . in the dumpster out back, but—" Mrs. Potter didn't get to finish because Tommy and Twig were squeezing through the door.

She walked back to her sewing machine and sat down. She pushed a lever with her foot and the machine whirred into action. Tommy and Twig burst back into the shop, and the machine stopped.

"It's empty!"

"I know," Mrs. Potter said, smiling. "You ran away before I finished. The trash was picked up this morning. Early."

16 | Trash Flash, Inc.

MONDAY 9:54 A.M.

Tommy's face turned the color of a boiled potato. Twig's jaw snapped shut.

"You boys okay?" Mrs. Potter asked.

No answer.

Mrs. Potter stood up. "Were those jeans . . . important?"

It was all over. Done, finished. No harm in telling the truth. "I had a lottery ticket in the pocket," Tommy said. "Worth a million dollars."

"A mil—"

"And I get half," Twig moaned. "*Got* half," he added.

Mrs. Potter sank into her chair. She took off her glasses, wiped them on her skirt, put them back on again. "You boys are kidding me, right?"

Tommy shook his head. "It was on TV Saturday night."

Mrs. Potter's face was doing interesting things. She was somewhere between laughing and crying. "I threw a million dollars in the Dipsy Dumpster."

No one said anything, or moved.

Mrs. Potter picked up a small booklet near the telephone, checked a number, then dialed. She waited a few seconds and handed the phone to Tommy.

"The trash collector," she whispered.

Tommy took the phone and put it to his ear. He heard a man's voice.

"Trash Flash, you bag it, we drag it."

Tommy didn't know what to do. He looked at the talking thing in his hand.

"Trash Flash . . . is anyone there?" the voice asked.

Mrs. Potter was nodding her head up and down. "Talk," she mouthed to Tommy.

Tommy's brain clicked on. "Did you pick up the trash behind Fanny's Tailor Shop this morning?" he asked.

"Nope."

"Nope!"

"My brother did," the voice said. "Today's his day on the truck. Got a problem?"

"Yes," Tommy said. Then he told the voice what was in the pocket of the jeans Mrs. Potter had thrown away.

Silence.

"Are you there?" Tommy asked.

"Yeah, I'm here. Did I hear you right just now?"

Tommy nodded. "Uh-huh. My fa—"

"Where are you calling from?"

"Fanny's Tailor Shop."

"Don't go anywhere," the voice said, and was gone.

Tommy handed the receiver back to Mrs. Potter. "I think they're coming here," he said.

Mrs. Potter hung up and nodded. Twig chewed his hair and blinked a lot. They looked out the windows at Fish Fry Street. Tommy asked if there was a bathroom.

They were still standing there ten minutes later when a green pickup roared to a stop out front. A yellow lightning bolt flashed across the door of the truck. Underneath, in orange, were the words *Trash Flash, Inc.*

A blond guy in his twenties jumped out of the driver's side and ran into the shop.

"Hi, I'm Rudy," he said. "My brother radioed me that someone here threw away a lottery ticket worth"—Rudy stopped to swallow—"a million bucks?"

Mrs. Potter spoke up. "It's in a pair of jeans that belong to this boy." She put her hand on Tommy's shoulder. "I threw them in the bin last night. They'd still have been there this morning."

Rudy nodded. "I was here about six o'clock and dumped that load about two hours ago." He grinned at Tommy and Twig. "You guys feel like going dump picking?"

Tommy wanted to go home to bed and pull the covers over his head, but he nodded.

"What about our bikes?" Twig asked.

"Toss 'em in the back of my truck." Rudy was moving toward the door.

"Thanks, Mrs. Potter," Tommy said. "I real—"

"Go!"

They went. Tommy and Twig shared the seat next to Rudy. He whipped a U-turn on two wheels and headed toward Main Street. From there he streaked across the intersection, barreled down the ramp and aimed his truck onto Interstate 91 going north.

Twig, sitting closest to Rudy, watched the speedometer. He elbowed Tommy. They both stared at the red needle.

"You guys ever been to the town dump?" Rudy asked.

"Unh-uh."

"I'm speeding because they bulldoze the stuff that gets dumped, cover it over with dirt." He glanced at his watch. "We could be too late already."

17 | Down in the Dump

MONDAY   10:10 A.M.

Tommy slumped back in the seat, as much as he could with Twig squished in next to him. His stomach heaved and settled.

A CB radio sputtered on the dashboard in front of him. The dash was covered with white fur. Twig stroked it with the back of his hand.

"Fake," Rudy said. "Looks real, though, doesn't it? Found it in the dump last summer, threw it in the washing machine, whammo, white again."

"Where's this dump?" Twig asked.

"Couple more minutes." They were headed north on the highway, leaving Hartford's skyline behind them. Rudy kept mashing down on the gas pedal, then easing it when they came up behind another driver he couldn't pass.

They passed a sign that said EAST-WEST SERVICE ROAD, NEXT RIGHT, and Rudy released the gas and downshifted. Then they were on another road, smaller and parallel to the highway they'd just left. They turned right again, this time onto a dirt road. Rudy spun the wheel to the left and they were climbing a hill. Dust flew up thickly all around the truck. The boys saw junk sticking out of the dirt on both sides of the narrow, rutted road.

"Is this it?" Tommy asked.

"This is where the dump used to be when the city first started putting trash here," Rudy explained. "But it keeps growing." He waved his arm out the window at the flat area all around them. "Everything you see is the old dump that's been covered over."

"You mean we're driving over stuff people threw away a long time ago?" Twig was impressed.

"Yep. The city keeps adding the new trash at the end of this road. They'll have to stop." Rudy pointed straight ahead toward a line of tall trees. "That's the Connecticut River behind those maples."

But Tommy wasn't looking at the trees. To the right of where Rudy pointed, he saw half a dozen huge white dump trucks in a line. The first one was vomiting up tons of trash, creating a mountain of garbage. The second was opening its giant jaws. As fast as the trash came tumbling out, a bulldozer pushed the stuff over a hill, making more room.

Tons of sand, in small dunes, lined the edge of the dumping area. Tommy and Twig watched the dozer blade rip into one of the dunes and begin spreading the sand, covering everything.

Off to the left, pickups like Rudy's and vans and station wagons were making a smaller mountain of rubbish. A few people scrambled over the piles, looking for thrown-away treasure.

A soft, hot breeze blew dust and bits of paper across the acres of sand-covered garbage. A rotten smell drifted through the windows, making Tommy and Twig pinch their noses till another breeze temporarily cleaned the air. Over-head, hundreds of sea gulls hovered, waiting for a chance to scavenge. Their screams made Tommy think of the beach.

Rudy had braked about fifty yards from the dumping area. Tommy sat stunned. How would he find anything in this mess? He shook his head. Some sea gull had probably eaten his lottery ticket by now.

"Where do we start?" Twig asked. He was trying to shove Tommy through the door.

"Wait here a minute." Rudy jumped from the cab and loped across the partially covered rubbish. He approached the dozer, cupped his mouth and shouted something to the driver. The machine stopped, and the operator hopped to the ground next to Rudy. They talked, pointing first to Rudy's truck, then to the mountain of trash, like actors in a silent movie. The operator climbed on the dozer again and Rudy started running back.

"Come on! Your jeans haven't been covered yet!"

Tommy and Twig hit the ground running. The bulldozer was moving toward the smaller vehicles. It stopped behind a van and the operator jumped down. "I won't let 'em dump any more while you're looking," he said to Rudy. He smiled at the boys. "Mind if I don't help? I don't want to be tempted!"

Rudy pointed to the spot where he'd dumped his first load that morning. "You'll have to look under everything. A lot more has been dumped since I was here." He thumped Tommy on the back. "I gotta take off, but I'll leave your bikes. I'll be thinking about you guys!"

Tommy and Twig watched the dust balloon up behind the pickup as it roared away. Tommy wondered if he'd ever see his parents again. He'd be stranded in this dump forever, forced to eat garbage and sleep on old smelly mattresses.

Twig grabbed his arm and pulled him toward the right pile. "I read in this magazine about some guy who built a house from stuff he found in the dump," Twig jabbered as they stumbled along.

"Except for windows. He never found any windows that weren't broken." Twig paused. "You know what Eskimos use for windows on their igloos? Walrus stomachs stretched tight. *Walrus stomachs!* If I was an Eskimo, know what I'd use? Plastic. Anyway, this guy—"

"Twig?"

"Yeah?"

"Shut up."

18 | Pirates

"Look at *this!* Man, how can people throw all this good stuff away?" Twig struggled to move a tire from on top of a broken but usable hockey game. This was the fourth treasure he'd discovered in a half hour. He laid the game next to his pile of goodies: a hatchet with cracked handle; a small motor; a shoe box filled with cassette tapes.

"Boy," Twig babbled, "I'm coming here again tomorrow. There's millions of good things here!"

Everything, Tommy thought blackly, except my jeans. He kicked a garbage bag, one of about a thousand he and Twig had already moved. They'd looked in and under every cardboard box and shoved aside every bag and barrel. They hadn't seen any jeans, let alone ones with paint on the knee, and he didn't know where else to look.

All Tommy had for his efforts was a headache. He yanked a small tree stump from a pile of branches and sat down. His pants and shirt were filthy with dump grime. Sweat and mosquitoes and flies fought over his eyes and ears. He was sure he stunk like the rest of the dump.

75

That's when he saw the other kids. There were three of them strolling toward Twig's pile of treasures.

The kid in the middle picked up one end of the hockey game and started dragging it away. Twig said something, and all three kids laughed. One of them swung the hatchet around his head, whooping like an Indian.

Tommy knew what Twig was going to do before he did it. Twig jumped in the air and landed with both feet on the hockey game, crushing the cheap metal.

The third kid jumped on Twig and threw him to the ground.

By the time Tommy got there, Twig was flat on his back in someone's old paper plates and napkins. The kid who jumped him had his hands locked on Twig's arms; one knee was planted in his stomach and the other pinned his chest, high, near the throat.

Twig was turning blue.

Tommy wrapped his arms around the kid's head and pulled. He was immediately sorry. He found himself on the ground staring up at a bunch of curious sea gulls.

When his eyes stopped chasing gulls, he realized the two heavy things on his chest were knees. The knees were blue because his attacker was wearing jeans. But one knee was partly white, where paint had slopped on it.

Tommy giggled. Then he laughed out loud. He laughed so hard, tears spurted out of the corners of his eyes and ran down his temples into his ears.

Twig sat up and gawked at Tommy. Then he laughed too, rocking and slapping his thighs.

"What's so funny?" The kid on Tommy's chest glanced at his buddies. "You see anything funny?"

"Maybe he hit his head and went nutso," the one with the hatchet said.

"They both look weird to me," said the kid who had jumped Twig. "Let's split. I didn't want that dumb game anyway."

The boy on top of Tommy gave him an extra shove and released him.

Tommy stood and wiped some of the crud from his seat and legs. He pointed at the jeans with the white knee. "You found those here in the dump, right?"

"What if I did?"

"They're mine."

"Tough for you."

"I don't want them," Tommy said, grinning like an idiot, "only what's in the pocket."

19 | Killer Scorpion

MONDAY   10:55 A.M.

"What's in the pocket?" The kid looked down. "I don't see nothin'."

"My pet scorpion." Tommy looked straight into the bully's eyes. "My mother accidentally knocked his cage over and Killer hid in the pocket of my jeans, so my mother threw them out."

"Scorpion!" The kid went rigid and his eyes bulged.

"Those things are poisonous, aren't they?" one of his pals asked.

Tommy nodded. "But he's probably asleep from the warmth." Tommy's eyes showed concern. "Just don't put your hand in there."

The kid's hands flew away from his thighs. His friends backed away a few feet.

Twig moved closer. "I think I saw it move," he whispered.

"What're you gonna do?" one of the others asked Tommy.

He scratched his head. "Guess I'll have to get another scorpion." He turned and started to walk away. "Come on," he said to Twig. "My mom'll kill me if I'm late for lunch."

"What about me?" The kid in Tommy's jeans hadn't moved a millionth of an inch. "You can't leave me here!"

Tommy stopped and turned around. "I got an idea," he said, "but you won't like it."

"What?" the kid said.

"Get rid of the jeans," Tommy said, grinning.

"I'd be in my underwear!" the kid blurted. "How would I get home?"

"Your problem." Tommy turned away and kept walking.

"Unless," the kid said, snapping his fingers at his friends, "you trade jeans with me."

Tommy stopped again. "Huh?"

"You gimme your jeans and you get your scorpion back."

Tommy was surrounded by the other two.

"Great idea!" Tommy sat down and untied his sneakers. He kicked them off and stripped down to his shorts, handing the jeans to Twig. They both watched the kid being lowered to the ground by his friends. No one said a word as he was helped out of the jeans.

The jeans were handed to Twig, who handed them over to Tommy.

When the trade was completed, Tommy checked the back pockets of the jeans. He grinned at Twig. "It's there all right."

He stepped into the jeans with the paint on the knee and they left to get their bikes.

They never even looked back.

20 | Rich!

WEDNESDAY

Two days later they were famous. The story took up half the front page of the *Hartford Courant*. The picture showed two grinning boys holding up a pair of blue jeans. One knee had white paint on it.

MILLION DOLLAR JEANS RECOVERED IN CITY DUMP

Thomas Archer, shown above with his best friend, Sydney Collins, is a millionaire today. Actually, Tommy is a half millionaire, as he split his fortune with his friend.

It seems that Tommy was given a lottery ticket as a gift. The ticket went into his jeans, and the jeans went to a rummage sale at his church. When the jeans were finally traced, they were in the dump, being worn by another boy. Asked how he persuaded the boy to give up the jeans, Tommy told this reporter it was a trade secret.

21 | Sunny Honolulu

SATURDAY   11:30 A.M.

"Tell me again how much." Twig sucked the pulp from a cherry and spit the seed into the grass.

"Fifty thousand a year before taxes." Tommy closed his eyes and a slow grin spread across his face. "For twenty years."

They were sitting at the picnic table under Twig's father's cherry tree. It was so hot, even their sweat was sweating.

"You mean they stop paying us"—Twig counted on his fingers—"when we're thirty? What're we supposed to do then?"

"Some people get jobs," Tommy said drily. "I'm putting mine in the bank. By the time I'm thirty, I'll have twice as much."

"My dad says I have to invest mine, too," Twig said glumly. "Until I'm twenty-one. What good is it to be a millionaire, if—"

"Half millionaire."

"—half millionaire, if I can't spend my dough?"

"Don't be so piggy. We're going to Hawaii, aren't we?" Tommy leaned back and stretched with his feet hooked under the picnic table. "Two weeks from now we'll be *surfing!*"

Twig leaped into the air and grabbed a branch of the cherry tree. "I'M GOING TO HAWAII!" He swung on the branch like a chimpanzee. "HEY, EVERYBODY, I'M GO-ING TO SUNNY HONOLULU!"

Mrs. Donkins popped up behind the hedge. "Is that yelling necessary, Sydney?"

"Sorry," Twig mumbled. He released the branch. "We're celebrating."

Mrs. Donkins stared over the hedge, blinking her blue eyes under her gardening hat. "I'm very happy for you both," she said in a softer voice. She cleared her throat. "Would some lemonade and cookies taste good?"

"Sure! Great," the boys said.

They watched Mrs. Donkins scurry up her back steps.

"She sure is nice today," Twig commented.

"Not only her," Tommy said. "I've gotten phone calls from people I don't even know."

Twig nodded. "Some guy in New York called my dad and asked if we wanted to invest in a Broadway play."

They heard Mrs. Donkins' back door slam. "Should we invite her to the party?" Twig whispered.

"Why not?"

She appeared again, with a tray holding a small pitcher of lemonade, two glasses and a plate of cookies. "Now don't drink it too fast," Mrs. Donkins said. "It's not good to gulp cold drinks in this heat."

Twig took the tray. "Thanks a lot, Mrs. Donkins. We're having a party tomorrow. Would you like to come?"

Mrs. Donkins smiled, and the smile changed her whole face. "Why, I'd love to. May I bring something?"

"I don't know, I think my mom's got everything organized, but you could call her."

"I will, Sydney, and thank you again."

"Mrs. Donkins?" Twig balanced on one foot while he scratched the back of his leg with the other foot. "Could you please call me Twig? I hate Sydney."

Mrs. Donkins smiled. "Twig it is. Just leave the things on my steps when you're finished."

The boys thanked her again and carried the tray to the picnic table.

"So how many does that make?" Tommy took a slug of his lemonade, ignoring Mrs. Donkins' advice.

"Over thirty, I think," Twig said, sinking his teeth into a chocolate-chip cookie.

Tommy grabbed a handful and chewed with his friend. The party was his idea, but because Twig's yard was bigger, they were having it there. Tommy wanted to get all the people together who had helped him find his jeans, plus a few others, including Muriel Morrow, the woman who bought him the lottery ticket. The boys' families had invited all the relatives within a hundred miles.

Tommy and Twig made a special trip to find Red Sally, but the rest had been invited over the phone. It was easy getting hold of Mr. Fallon, Mr. and Mrs. Potter, and Rudy and his brother, and the others. But they hadn't known Muriel's name until Tommy had received her letter the day before.

Tommy had hustled over to Twig's house and read him the letter.

Dear Tommy,

*Thank you again for returning my
wallet. I read about your good luck
in the newspaper. It couldn't have
happened to a nicer person. Here are
two tickets for my show. I hope you can
make it, and bring your cute girlfriend
with the red hair.*

Sincerely,
Muriel Morrow

Muriel had the lead in the Hartford Stage Company
production of *Dance with Me, Baby*. She had gotten Tommy's address and name from the newspaper. When he
received her tickets, Tommy called and invited Muriel to
the party.

"What're you wearing tonight?" Tommy asked.

"I don't know." Twig nibbled at a cookie. "I've never
been to a real play before, only the dumb ones at school.
Maybe I won't go, anyway," he added.

Tommy laughed. "You still mad at her for calling you
my girlfriend? How was she supposed to know? Maybe
where she comes from boys don't have long hair." He
grabbed Twig's cheek and gave it a little tug. "You are
kind of pretty."

Twig swatted Tommy's hand away. "I'm thinking of getting it cut, anyway."

"Why?" Tommy was amazed. "You've always had long
hair."

"Mom says when we go on that TV show I have to look
respectable."

Tommy shook his head. "All they're gonna do is ask us what it feels like to be millionaires."

"Still." Twig finished off the last cookie. "Besides, if I leave it long, seaweed and junk will get in it when we're skin-diving in Hawaii." He punched Tommy on the arm.

"Yeah, I can't wait," Tommy sighed. "And if it hadn't been for Muriel dropping her wallet, none of this would have happened."

Twig found another cookie crumb. "How're we getting to the play tonight?"

"My dad's driving us. Don't forget the tickets."

"Tickets?" Twig stared at Tommy. "You have the tickets."

Tommy shook his head. "I brought them over when I showed you Muriel's letter, remember?"

"No you didn't. You brought the letter and I asked you where the tickets were. You said they were home."

"OH MY GOD!" Tommy leaped off the bench and headed out of Twig's yard.

"Where're you going?"

"To get the tickets out of my pocket," Tommy yelled over his shoulder. "Mom's doing the laundry today!"